C000172024

RIDE SHARE STRIPPER

GAY PUBLIC SEX SERIES #6

NICO FOX

CONTENTS

CHAPTER 1

MY NAME IS Bryce and I've been driving Uber for two years. It's not my main job. I have a paid internship at a software company that pays a pittance, and I need this side gig to keep myself in my studio apartment.

I have seen my share of crazy ass things. There are so many stories to tell, that I could write 50 books about it.

I've had passengers crying after a big breakup, fighting with each other and breaking up in front of me.

I've even had a guy propose to his fiancée in my car. Can you believe that? He got down on one knee, partially, and took out the ring right there while I was waiting for the light to turn red.

I once had a CEO demeaning one of his employees who he then fired right there in my car, with more than 20 minutes of driving to go. Freaking awkward!

And then there's the sex. It's very common for people to want to join what I call the "Mile Long Club," as opposed to the "Mile High Club," when people have sex and airplanes. I just made that term up – don't know what else to call it. The point is, people want to get it on in my backseat.

I do my best not to laugh when it happens, and I usually get a huge tip for keeping my mouth shut.

Technically, this is prohibited, and illegal, but I care more about pleasing my customers and getting big tips. If they want to do the nasty while going 65 mph, I say go for it. Just clean up afterwards. I even keep a container of disinfectant wipes for them.

One woman contacted me three months after banging her husband in my backseat and told me that I helped her to conceive her child. She named the kid after me. What an honor!

It doesn't hurt that I get a little peek here and there of the hot guys as they drop their pants and their wives, girlfriends, mistresses, or even hookers go down on them. It makes my job just that much more bearable. Even better when it's a gay couple.

Not that I'm innocent either. I've had a little tryst here and exchanged a phone number there and even gotten the date out of it.

I can never be the one to make the first move. If I hit on a guy and he's not interested, and he reports me because I make him feel uncomfortable, I would be in so much trouble.

At best, I'd lose my Uber driving privileges. At worst, I'd be arrested.

Don't get me wrong, most rides are ho-hum. Being an Uber driver isn't a world of wild excitement. Most of it is spent in heavy traffic and every once in a while you get a real jerk, a bunch of drunks, or if you're really unlucky, somebody throws up in your car.

Only rarely does it get hot and steamy, and even rarer to I get to be involved in the action. But it pays the bills.

Tonight was just an average Friday night. I've been driving for eight hours so I was pretty tired. In between rides, I would search for Grindr hookups, looking for a guy who went to the bars, got a little tipsy, but didn't get lucky. That's when I'm most likely to score.

The story I'm about to tell you, is about the wildest sex of my life. I swear to God, I'm not making this up. Nor am I bragging or embellishing.

It was approximately two in the morning, and I am driving two college-aged women home from one of the popular bars back to their dorm rooms at the local university.

It was an Uber pool, so I went to pick up a third rider at a strip club for women.

"Maybe we should go to the strip club instead," said the blonde directly behind me.

"I wish," said the other blonde in the other seat. "We're about 15 minutes too late. They close at two."

"Damn," said the other. They both giggled a little bit, and I joined in on the fun.

"Maybe the new passenger will be one of the hot strippers."

It's always possible. I'd picked up passengers from this club before, and it was definitely not a gay strip club.

The only people there are the male strippers and female patrons. The rider I was picking up was listed as Alex J.

I waited for a good 10 minutes until I became impatient. Just as I was about to cancel, a guy that looked like a fucking statue of an ancient Greek God came into view.

He was looking at his phone and then around at all the cars passing by, as if he were looking for me. I flashed my signal and waved to him.

He knocked on the front passenger side window. "Are you Bryce, the Uber driver?" he asked in a deep baritone voice.

I nodded yes, while the women in the back giggles some more. He was hot. Like ridiculously freaking hot. Like he had to be a stripper because what else would you do with that body?

He wore a muscle shirt that barely cringed to his chest, track pants that were about five sizes too small, and a pair of trainers on his feet.

"Do you want me to sit in the front or squeeze in the back with these two?" He pointed to the two women who would not stop giggling.

Before I could respond, one of the women said, "In back! In back with us! I'll sit on his lap."

He rolled his eyes, and I said, "Whatever you'd like."

He got in the front seat, much to the disappointment of my other riders. I did my best to not gawk at his balls, but, come on!

It's like they were popping out of those things and about to hit me in the face. It's like he wanted people to look at it. In the two women kept glancing over their seat to get a better view.

They kept bombarding him with questions like, "Are you a stripper there?" And, "Would you do a private lap dance for me in my dorm room?"

I pulled up to the dorm hall and had to beg the women to get out at their stop and stop harassing my other rider. He nodded politely, but I could tell he was fed up with it.

After they got out, I pulled away toward his destination. I was a little nervous around someone so fucking hot.

"Every Friday and Saturday night, I get drunk people from the bars acting all silly and horny," I said.

"That's how it was all night at the club. I had three bachelorette parties to dance for," he sighed.

I bet you like the attention. And you have your pick of those horny ladies." I wanted to test his reaction.

He huffed. "Yeah right. Not my thing, if you know what I mean." He turned to look at me. I gave him a moment of eye contact, but I didn't want to keep my eyes off the road for too long.

"Even if it was my thing, if a dancer slept with a patron, they'd be fired on the spot. Some guys have done it though and gotten away with it because nobody found out."

"That's how it is for Uber drivers too. We be fired if we slept with a rider." I looked back at him and then at his bulge, trying to remember that I was driving.

5

He laughed. "That's only if somebody found out." He raised his eyebrows at me.

I liked where this was going. It's always a thrill to be hit on by a rider, but this guy was hot enough to be a professional stripper.

My concentration was shot, and I swerved out of my lane a little. "Sorry," was all I could say as I straightened the car out.

"Looks like you had a little bit to drink tonight."

"Me?" I asked. "Not while on the job. Not while driving. Just got a little distracted, that's all."

"I haven't had a lick to drink either, but my mind is swirling in anticipation." He put his hand on my thigh.

CHAPTER 2

HIS EYES INVITED ME IN. I glanced back and forth between him and the road ahead. He shifted in the passenger seat and slid his hand toward my crotch. I was going about 70 mph.

I reached over to grab him as well. Our arms crossed over the elbow rest between the two seats. I pulled it out so I would have easier access.

His long spongy member filled up in my hand. Now I could see why he was a stripper. It had to be 6 inches completely flaccid.

He swirled his hips as if he were fucking my hand. He wanted it bad.

"You like my cock?" he asked, playfully.

"I'm here to please you. I'm all about excellent customer service."

"We should find a place where we can play so you don't drive us off the road."

"I once took a guy to the 12th Avenue bridge, near the Fillmore Auditorium," Alex said. "Total amount of privacy under trees. We'd never get caught."

I mock yawned. "Boring. What's the fun in that?"

"You *want* to get caught?" His eyes widened.

"You're the stripper. You're the one who likes the thrill of being half-naked while people ogle you," I said.

He pretended to look shy, as if he wasn't aware that he had a seductive effect on strangers drooling over his body.

He gave a wide grin. "Yeah, maybe. You're pretty hot too." I couldn't fricking believe that a stripper was calling me hot. And he wasn't even trying to get me to put more bills in his G-string.

"I'm not *dance in front of screaming ladies* hot though," I said. He looked down, as if he were embarrassed. "Besides, there's a place I've always wanted to try." He gave me a questionable look.

"A week ago, I got a flat going north on I-25 near the stadium," I continued. "I called the towing company, but they told me it'd be an hour. I was parked on the shoulder of the interstate just scrolling through Facebook and eventually I switched to porn. Traffic passed me by as I jerked off. I thought it might a great place to take one of my special riders."

"Special riders? So, you've done this before?"

"Don't slut shame me." I said while laughing. "Besides, you're the one who takes his clothes off for money."

"Touché!" We both laughed.

I pulled off the exit that went onto the interstate. After about 5 minutes, I found an area where the shoulder was wider than it was on the rest of the road. Last thing I wanted was to be accidentally hit by another driver while giving a blow job.

"We can't do that here?" Alex looked around at the cars going by. "We'll get caught."

"Nah, don't worry. People are going by, but nobody is paying attention."

I took the foot off the gas and coasted to my chosen spot.

Let me just pause this ride on the Uber app. I called AAA, the company I'd call if my car was really broken down, just in case I needed the evidence later. Every time the flicker of a car's headlights passed by, a surge of adrenaline rushed through my veins.

My cock throbbed as I unzipped my jeans and undid the button to tease him. I pulled his pants all the way down to his ankles to reveal my trophy.

It was a massive, thick, and hard as fuck piece of meat. I buried my face deep into it. The ripeness drew me in and I fondled is low orbs.

I imagined all the women that wanted this prize. How they must have screamed when he came on stage to shake his thing.

How all those women must have grabbed at it and tried to get a peak. How they must have gone home and made love to their husbands but fantasized about Alex. I wanted it all for myself.

I sat back up to look around. Wanted to make sure we were safe. Some cars slowed down to see what was going on with my car, thinking I was just stuck.

Little did they know Alex was tugging my pants down to the brake pedal while my hand was circling his pre-come around his mushroom head.

My dick swelled, and he started to give me a hand job, or at least the best he could with me leaning over while I blew him.

Then he stopped.

"Oh shit, oh shit, oh shit!" Alex was breathing heavy in panic. "Cops."

I sat up again and looked back. Red and blue lights flashed in my eyes.

CHAPTER 3

I HYPERVENTILATED.

"Pull up your pants and act as if nothing strange is happening."

I leaned down and slowly zipped own pants up to look as nonchalant as possible, like anything other than I was getting dressed.

He pulled his up the best he could. The combination of his huge cock and thin track pants made it painfully obvious that he was hard as a rock.

"And cover your dick with your arm. You look like a stripper."

The police officer sat in his car for a couple of minutes before getting out. Alex and I said nothing as the cop walked towards us.

"License and registration." I pulled them out from the compartment beneath the elbow rest and gave them to the officer. "What's wrong with your car?"

"It's overheated again. I think. I had the same problem last week. Something with the carburetor or transmission or one of those things that go putt-putt. I called AAA and they're sending someone now."

I pulled out my phone and showed him my call history that had AAA as the most recent call. Good thing I did that.

The officer looked at me and then at Alex and then back and forth several times. He seemed to notice that Alex was hiding something.

"Drop it!" The cop yelled as he pulled out his gun and pointed it towards us. We both put our hands in the air, and Alex couldn't hide his noticeably hard dick anymore.

The officer laughed and put his gun away. "Sorry. I thought you might be hiding a gun. That's not a gun, is it?" He laughed some more. "But it's definitely a weapon." He gave two comical winks at Alex. "Bet the ladies like you."

"More than you know," Alex said, relaxing and joining in on the laughing.

"Ok, you two. Take care and good luck with your car. Make sure not to get out of the car until the tow truck gets here. You want to stay safe on this busy highway."

The officer handed my license back to me. "And you!" He pointed at Alex. "Stay away from my wife!" He laughed and walked back to his car.

Neither of us made a move for a good 5 minutes. When the coast was clear, my hand moved back to his crotch.

Something about almost being caught gave me such a rush. My heart was beating fast and Alex's tank of a chest moved up and down with his breathing.

Now was the time to claim my prize. I yanked his pants down and savored the length of him. As I stared at his cock, he was relaxed and confident. It must be normal for him when people fixate on his dick.

I could only take half of him in my mouth. My hand wrapped around the base. I bobbed my head up and down, moving my hand in tandem. I hummed on his dick and I could tell from his response that he liked it.

After a good couple of minutes, his breathing increased and so did the width of his cock. I could barely breathe without choking.

Alex pushed my head back. "I don't want to finish in your mouth. I want to finish inside you."

I pulled my jeans all the way off and threw them in the back seat. Pretty risky, given that the cops had already checked on us. My skin stuck to the black leather seats.

The breeze blew through the crack in the window, hitting my exposed crotch. I felt vulnerable. Exposed. Open.

"Get on me."

I wasn't sure what he was getting at. Car sex is always difficult. There's more room to maneuver in the back seat. In the front you have to limit yourself to oral.

But he waved his come-hither hand, and I crawled on top of him in the passenger seat. I steadied myself by holding on to his indestructible biceps.

If any cars driving by looked close enough, they could see my bare ass and maybe a glimpse of my dick.

I sat on his massive tree-trunk thighs just below his cock.

"How do you want to do this?"

"I lift, you spread."

"Huh?"

Then he picked me up with ease and held my body over him, like I was a toy doll. He moved me up and down with little effort, easing the edge of my ass with his cock.

I grabbed lube out of the glove compartment and spread my cheeks. He lowered me slowly, opening and filling me, and then lifted me again until only his mushroom head remained inside. Then he thrust me down onto his cock.

I had a fleeting moment of pain followed by intense pleasure. His dick reached deeper in my canal than any other guy had. My prostate never had this much pressure on it and my ass tightened its grip around him.

My hands reached behind me to rub his torso. I ran them over his tight abs, and he tugged his shirt which he lifted over his head and threw to the side.

I trembled. Every nerve ending in my body seemed to be on fire. My cock was straining and peeking out as if flopped up and down on the dashboard.

If someone were watching us in the daytime, they would have a clear view of my dick. All I could do was let out a moan.

My mind completely shut down and wandered into a forest of passion. I was in a trance. A moment of clarity. It was almost a spiritual experience.

I wasn't even touching my cock, but I felt the most intense pleasure I'd ever seen. It took over my whole body.

He was at a breaking point too. His cock expanded to fill my whole canal.

As he climaxed, I felt a buzzing electricity throughout my body. I came at the same time shooting several bursts onto the dashboard and even hitting the windshield. The wave ran over me multiple times.

We sat in the seat, trying to catch our breaths. His deep breathing felt like the car was moving.

I grabbed tissues out of the glove compartment and cleaned off the come from the windshield and eased myself off him and back into the driver's seat.

"I hope the traffic surveillance camera didn't catch us," I said while pointing to the telephone pole with one on it.

His shoulders tightened, and he said nothing.

I laughed. "Don't worry. I picked this location for a reason."

"You really have planned this all out."

"Yup. Planned out the scenarios, just didn't have the part-ner." I rubbed my hand over his chest one more time. "I hope you'll give me a 5-star rating."

We drove the rest of the way to his apartment in silence.

"Why don't you stop by the club tomorrow night and I can give you a private dance. At the club they call me Valentino."

His stripper name was almost as hot as his body.

"I'll be there with plenty of bills."

I checked the app to see if he rated me. He gave me a $50 tip for a $20 ride.

One day, when I write a book about my experiences as an Uber driver, the chapter on Alex, or shall I say, Valentino, will be the final climax of the book.

I doubt I'll have a better story to tell than this one.

ABOUT THE AUTHOR

Hi, I'm Nico. I love to write gay stories about public sex, cruising, bathhouses, anything taboo and a little bit dirty.

When I'm not writing, I love hanging out at the bars and binge-watching Netflix alike.

If you enjoyed this book, sign up for the Mailing List and receive a FREE book.

See you next time

-Nico

Join the Mailing List

For more information:
www.NicoFoxAuthor.com

ALSO BY NICO FOX

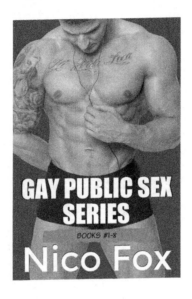

The complete Gay Public Sex Series box set. **Eight** steamy M/M erotic stories full of **public** encounters.

This bundle includes:

Bulge on a Train

Truck Stop Fantasy

Fitting Room Temptation

Ferris Wheel Threesome

Hole in the Wall Exhibitionist

Ride-Share Stripper

Gay Resort Weekend

Art Gallery Awakening

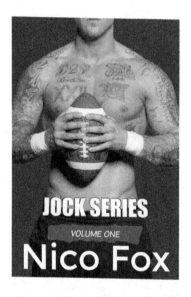

The first Jock Series box set. **Six** steamy M/M erotic stories full
of **sweaty athletic guys**.

This bundle includes:

Captain of the Swim Team

First Time, First Down

Soccer Jockstrap

Slammed By the Team

Team Catcher

Heavyweight Punch

The first DILF Series box set. Six stories about **hot daddies** and their younger counterparts.

This bundle includes:

DILF of My Dreams

Seduced by the DILF

My Boss is a DILF

First Time Gay with My Girlfriend's Dad

My Girlfriend's Dad Wants It

First Time Gay with the DILF Professor

CRUSH ON MY STRAIGHT BEST FRIEND
Nico Fox

"I always follow his lead about anything and everything. All of our friends do. He uses his charm and imposing stature to convince us to do anything he wants."

Finn always had a crush on his best friend, Cameron, who is *very* popular with the girls. Standing next to well-built, captain of the football team, and all-around stud Cameron makes Finn feel a little, shall we say, less than…insecure.

Cameron has always protected Finn from others when they make fun of him for his small stature and he's always felt secure with him.

Finn invites Cameron over for a night of video games and beer only to be shocked when Cameron makes a wager on a game that Finn can't say no to. Who says fantasies don't come true?

My BOSS for Christmas

Nico Fox

Dustin has landed his dream job in Silicon Valley just one month after graduating college. He tries to keep his head down as much as he can, despite being surrounded by **hyper-masculine alphas** that call each other ***bro.*** He just can't stop lusting after the company's founder, notorious womanizer and billionaire's son, Brett.

The company is in peril. A bug in their software may cause one of their biggest customers to leave them. Everyone in the office is nervous, but they try to cover it up with heavy drinking after work and carrying on with their secret Santa ritual.

But Dustin solves the bug, making him the company hero. Brett is eternally grateful to his new employee for saving his company. Find out how this straight stud will pay back his employee in this new erotic story from Nico Fox.

Angels and Devils

Nico Fox

A SEXY underground Halloween party...

"It's amazing how far two people in love will go to hide their inner desires from each other."

Lucas is a shy college student. His boyfriend, Colton, is an extroverted sports stud that every guy on campus wants to get with. Together, they have the perfect relationship. Or so it seems.

Lucas is worried someone will steal Colton away because he's such a catch. What's more, Lucas doesn't know if he can trust himself to handle monogamy.

They head into Manhattan to look for the perfect Halloween costumes for their upcoming school party. They want sexy costumes to show off all that hard work in the gym.

At the costume store, they meet Ace, a sophisticated New Yorker throwing his own Halloween party, one where inhibitions are thrown to the wind.

Ace seems a little shady. The party is so elusive that they need to be blindfolded as they ride in a limo to the party. But that's the price Lucas is willing to pay to go to a real New York City party.

How will Lucas and Colton's relationship hold up after a wild night at the party? Will jealousy get in the way, or will exploration bring their relationship to new heights?